CATS CAN

WORDS BY
ROSEANNE GREENFIELD THONG

PICTURES BY
EBONY GLENN

VIKING

VIKING
An imprint of Penguin Random House LLC, New York

First published in the United States of America by Viking,
an imprint of Penguin Random House LLC, 2022

Visit us online at penguinrandomhouse.com.

Library of Congress Cataloging-in-Publication Data is available.

Manufactured in China

ISBN 9780593115596

1 3 5 7 9 10 8 6 4 2

TOPL

Design by Opal Roengchai
Text set in Avenir
The illustrations were created digitally.

To my dear friend Wendy, who has fostered hundreds of cats
for Long Beach Spay & Neuter Foundation
until loving homes could be found for them. — R. G. T.

To all furry companions, and especially
my favorite ginger tabby, Archie.
— E. G.

Cats purr,
cats dream,

cats meow,

cats scream!

You bring them food—
it's all in vain.
They're sidetracked by
their toys again.

Cats leave their plate—
cats shrug their back.
But cats aren't shy
when it's time for a snack!

Cats love gymnastics,
so it seems.
They make good use
of balance beams!

They twirl, they stretch, they somersault,
though accidents are not their fault.

Boxes, from a kitten's view,
are just the place for peekaboo!

Hideouts made of cardboard walls
are castles, forts, and manor halls.

Cats don't really care for chores.
They'd rather topple chests and drawers.

And when you try to make the bed,
they fix that plan—and play instead.

Cats won't give up
a cozy nook.
The front yard is their
favorite book.

Charmed by squirrels and
sudden showers,
cats like to stare
outside for hours.

Cats never ever knock on doors.
They make themselves at home on floors.

Blocking hallways is their mission.
It's their house—who needs permission?

Cats purr, cats dream,
cats wake up to plan and scheme.

Cats help themselves without a peep.
Cats prowl when it is time for sleep!

Now and then, cats like to share,
though cat gifts can bring much despair.

Your favorite scarf brings cats much joy.
But let's be clear—it's not their toy!

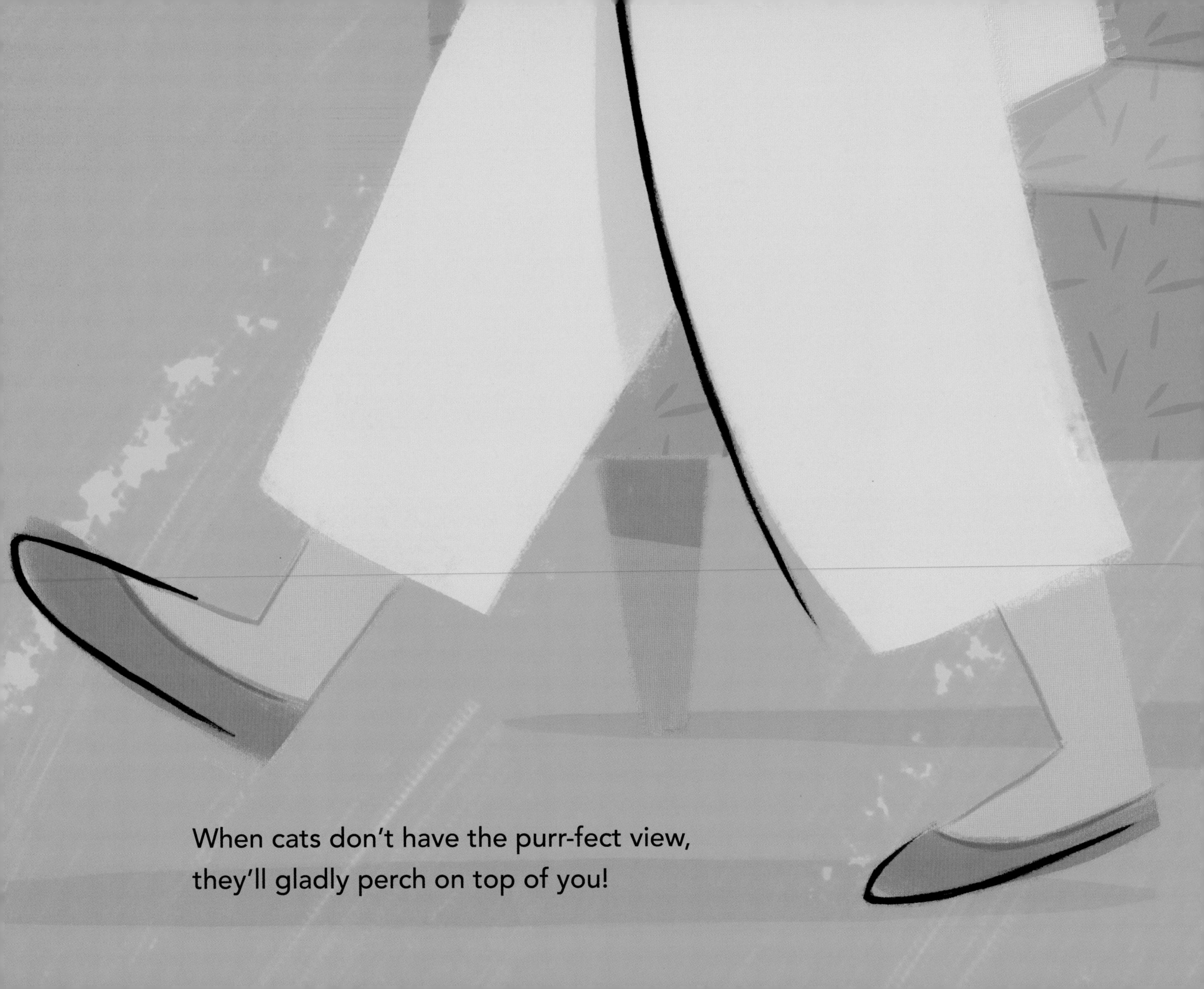

When cats don't have the purr-fect view,
they'll gladly perch on top of you!

Cats don't believe in wasting space.
Cats feel at home most every place!

Cats are tricky, cats are spry.

Cats can make you laugh and cry!

Cats win you over with their smile.

Cats can charm, cats can beguile.

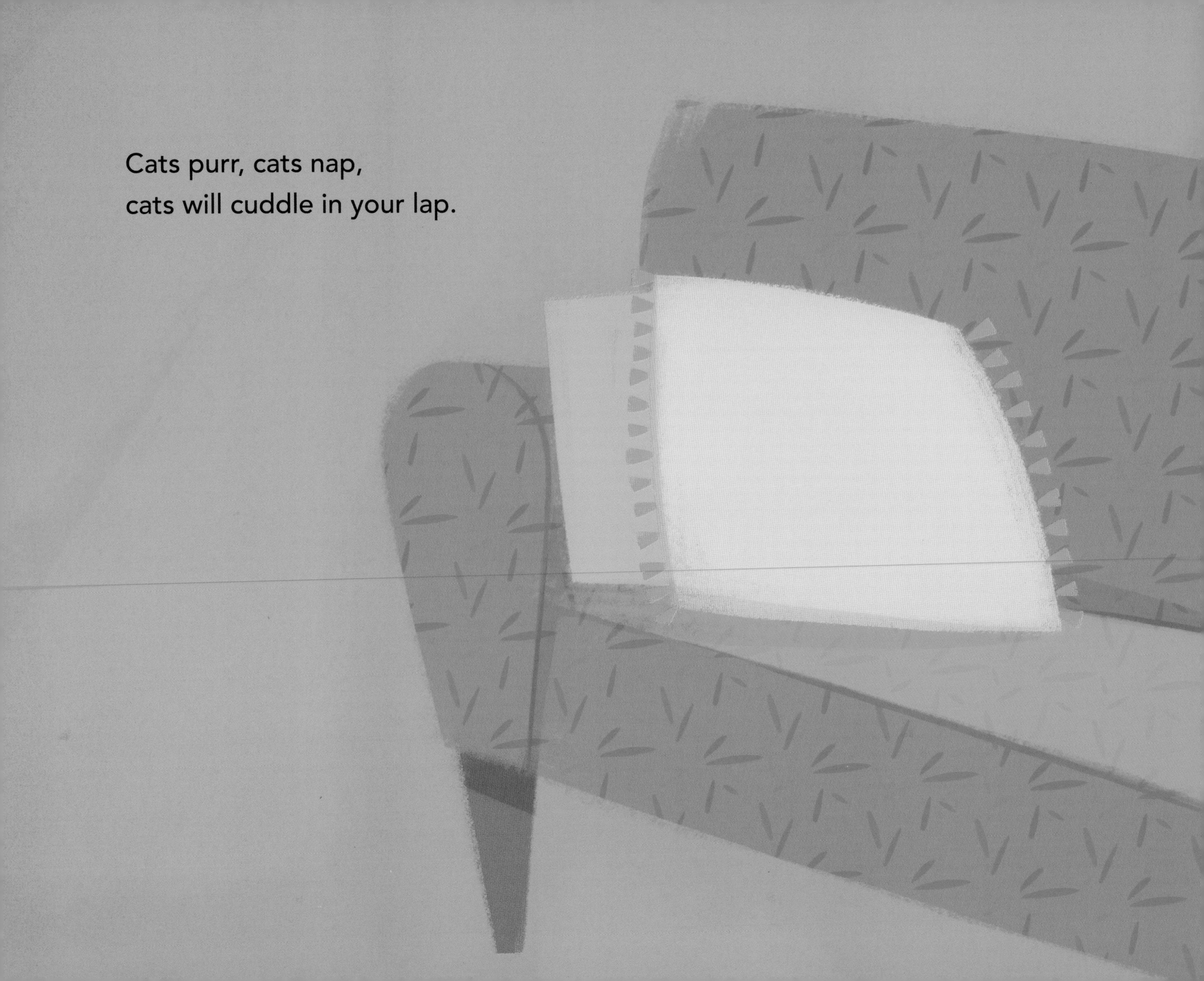
Cats purr, cats nap,
cats will cuddle in your lap.

Cats must be kissed
and be embraced.

Cats can never
be replaced!